My Mum Can't See

Written by Louise John
Illustrated by Andy Elkerton

WAYLAND

My mum can't see.

My Mum
Can't See

First published in 2010
by Wayland

This paperback edition published in 2011 by Wayland

Text copyright © Louise John
Illustration copyright © Andy Elkerton

Wayland
338 Euston Road
London NW1 3BH

Wayland Australia
Level 17/207 Kent Street
Sydney, NSW 2000

Series Editor: Louise John
Editor: Katie Powell
Cover design: Paul Cherrill
Design: D.R.ink
Consultant: Shirley Bickler

A CIP catalogue record for this book is available from the British Library.

ISBN 9780750260107 (hbk)
ISBN 9780750260145 (pbk)

Printed in China

Wayland is a division of Hachette Children's Books,
an Hachette UK Company

www.hachette.co.uk

But my mum likes
to play...

and my mum likes
to read.

My mum likes to walk...

and my mum likes
to jump!

My mum likes
to bake...

and my mum likes
to eat cake!

My mum can't see...

but my mum can
hug me!

Guiding a First Read of
My Mum Can't See

It is important to talk through the book with the child before they read it alone. This prepares them for the way the story unfolds, and allows them to enjoy the pictures as you both talk naturally, using the language they will later encounter when reading. Read them the brief overview below, and then follow the suggestions.

1. Talking through the book
This girl tells us about her mum. Her mum can't see but she likes to do lots of things that other mums do, and sometimes the girl helps her.

Let's read the title: **My Mum Can't See**
Now we'll look at the pictures.
On page 4, the girl says, "My mum can't see."
Turn to the next page.
"But," she says, "my mum likes to play."
There she is, playing with Lego.
Next page says, "My mum likes to read."
She has special books with bumps that she can feel to read.

Continue through the book, guiding the discussion to fit the text as the child looks at the illustrations.

On page 18, the girl says, "My mum can't see..."
Now, turn the page, "but my mum can...?"
Yes, she can "hug me!"

2. A first reading of the book

Ask the child to read the book independently, pointing carefully under each word (tracking), while thinking about the story. Praise attempts by the child to correct themselves, and prompt them to use their letter knowledge, the punctuation and check the meaning, for example:

> You said, "My mum can see." Does that make sense? Try it again. Good. Why did you change it? Did you spot the 't' on the end of 'can'? Well done.

> 'Likes to cook' makes sense but read it again carefully. Yes, that word does start with 'b'. It says 'bake'. Does that fit?

3. Follow-up activities

The high frequency words in this title are:

and   like   mum   my   to

- Select a new high frequency word, and ask the child or group to find it throughout the book. Discuss the shape of the letters and the letter sounds.
- To memorise the word, ask the child to write it in the air, then write it repeatedly on a whiteboard or on paper, leaving a space between each attempt.

4. Encourage

- Reading the book again – with expression.
- Drawing a picture based on the story.
- Writing one or two sentences using the practised words.

START READING is a series of highly enjoyable books for beginner readers. **The books have been carefully graded to match the Book Bands widely used in schools.** This enables readers to be sure they choose books that match their own reading ability.

Look out for the Band colour on the book in our Start Reading logo.

The Bands are:

Pink Band 1A & 1B

Red Band 2

Yellow Band 3

Blue Band 4

Green Band 5

Orange Band 6

Turquoise Band 7

Purple Band 8

Gold Band 9

START READING books can be read independently or shared with an adult. They promote the enjoyment of reading through satisfying stories supported by fun illustrations.

Louise John is really the editor of Start Reading, but wanted to see how she liked writing books, too. It was quite tricky, but she found that eating lots of chocolate biscuits made her think better! She tries out her ideas on her daughter, Amelia, who tells her if they are any good or not!

Andy Elkerton spent three years at art college before becoming an artist in the world of computer games. Eventually he escaped and now spends his time illustrating children's books like these.